STAR TREK IV ®

THE VOYAGE HOME

Cover Art and Text Copyright © 1986 by Paramount Pictures
Corporation.
All Rights Reserved, including the right of reproduction in whole or in
part in any form.
This Book is Published by Simon & Schuster, Inc., under exclusive
license from Paramount Pictures Corporation, the trademark owner.
A Byron Preiss Visual Publications, Inc. book. Published by
WANDERER BOOKS, A Divison of Simon & Schuster, Inc., Simon &
Schuster Building, 1230 Avenue of the Americas, New York, New York
10020.
STAR TREK is a Registered Trademark of Paramount Pictures
Corporation. WANDERER and colophon are registered trademarks of
Simon & Schuster, Inc.
Designed by Alex Jay. Edited by David M. Harris.
Manufactured in the United States of America.

ISBN: 0-671-63243-4   10 9 8 7 6 5 4 3 2 1

STAR TREK IV

THE VOYAGE HOME

By PETER LERANGIS

Screenplay by Steve Meerson & Peter Krikes
and Harve Bennett & Nicholas Meyer

Story by Leonard Nimoy & Harve Bennett

A Byron Preiss Book

A Wanderer Book
Published by Simon & Schuster, Inc., New York

It began with a sound. Nothing very frightening . . . just a harmless sort of gibberish.

But because no one could answer it, the future of the planet Earth was doomed.

The first victim was the Starship *Saratoga*. As the crew listened to the strange sound, they watched a huge probe float closer and closer. No matter what they tried, they

could not figure out how to answer it.

So the sound became louder—and suddenly the ship began to lose power. The science officer turned to the captain. "All systems have failed. We have reserve power only."

"We're out of control! Rig for collision!" the captain ordered.

The probe came closer to the ship. The

crew gasped when they saw it was miles long. But it just passed by harmlessly into the distance.

The science officer was stunned. "They finished us," he said. "And we don't even know what they want."

The place: Starfleet Federation Headquarters, San Francisco, USA, Earth. The time: the twenty-third century. In the Council Chamber, leaders from many planets were gathered. Among them was Sarek, father of Captain Spock. On the screen, a film of grave importance had begun.

A horrified hush came over the room as they all watched the USS *Enterprise* exploding to bits in outer space. When the film ended, another one immediately began.

"There! Hold the image!" The Klingon ambassador pointed at the screen, as a picture of the *Enterprises*'s Admiral Kirk appeared. "Behold the terrorist James T. Kirk! Not only is he responsible for murdering a Klingon crew and stealing a Klingon vessel. See now the *real* plot and intentions. . . ."

The film continued—the infamous
"Genesis film." On it, Kirk described the
most wondrous—and dangerous—process
ever known to the universe. Developed by

Kirk's son, the Genesis energy force could turn dead matter into life.

During the *Enterprise*'s battle with the great Khan, a Genesis pod was shot into a dead planet. Soon the planet teemed with jungles and lakes. Khan was beaten, but only after Spock died to save the *Enterprise*. A saddened crew sent Spock's corpse to rest on the Genesis planet.

Before long the Klingons arrived at the planet to steal the secret of Genesis. And as part of their plot, they murdered the son of Admiral Kirk.

As revenge, Kirk destroyed the *Enterprise*—but only after beaming the Klingon crew aboard, while he and his crew beamed down to Genesis.

The Klingon ambassador shouted: "Even as the Federation negotiated a peace treaty with us, Kirk was secretly developing Genesis! He created this planet—a base from which to launch the destruction of the Klingon people! We demand justice!"

The audience murmured as Sarek spoke: "Ambassador, Genesis was the creation of *life*, not death. It was the Klingons who destroyed the USS *Grissom* while trying to gain the secret of Genesis. And your men killed Kirk's son. Do you deny these events?"

"We have the right to preserve our race!"

"Do you have the right to murder?" Sarek asked evenly.

The Council President then turned to the Klingon. "Mr. Ambassador, the Council's deliberations are over. You have been allowed to put your views on record."

"Then Kirk goes unpunished?" the ambassador shouted.

"Admiral Kirk has been charged with nine violations of Starfleet regulations—"

"*Starfleet regulations?*" The ambassador looked furiously at the President. "Remember this well: There will be no peace as long as Kirk lives!" With that, he and his staff stormed out.

The President turned to the elder Vulcan. "Sarek, we ask you to return Kirk and his crew to answer for their crimes."

"With all respect, Mr. President," Sarek answered, "there is only *one* crime: denying Kirk and his crew the honors they so richly deserve."

"You are welcome to remain and testify," the President said as he ended the meeting.

Light-years away, on the planet Vulcan, Kirk and his crew had just finished an important project—creating a new spaceship to replace the destroyed *Enterprise.* And they had made it out of a captured Klingon vessel. Its new name: the HMS *Bounty.*

They were also waiting to find out if Spock was normal again. After Spock's death, his coffin had landed on the Genesis planet. As the dead planet was brought to life, so too was Spock—as a newborn baby. But Genesis had a flaw—everything aged much too fast, and Spock grew to manhood in less than a day. Kirk and his crew rescued him and brought him to Vulcan in the Klingon ship. But there was a problem: How could Spock possibly regain all the knowledge he had in his first life?

Spock had thought of that even before he died. Secretly, he had transferred everything in his mind to Doctor McCoy. Getting it back was another story. Only in Vulcan legend had memory ever been transferred back to someone who gave it away. But Spock and McCoy decided to risk their lives to try it. And they weren't sure it had worked.

The air was tense around the crew that once rode the *Enterprise*. Kirk spoke into his recorder:

"Captain's log, Stardate 8390. We are in our third month on Vulcan, awaiting the progress of Captain Spock's memory training. We have voted unanimously to return to Earth to face the consequences of our actions in the rescue of our comrade Spock." He turned to Mr. Scott. "How soon can we get underway?"

"Give me one more day, sir. Reading Klingon is hard."

Kirk nodded. Then he gazed away toward a tall Vulcan mountain. His eyes were filled with hope and fear.

On that mountain, Spock sat in a chamber, surrounded by three computer screens. His memory test was underway. With lightning speed, he answered all questions correctly—until the final one:

HOW DO YOU FEEL? flashed onto the screens.

"I do not understand," said Spock.

"Spock," a voice said. He turned to face his mother, Amanda. "The computer knows you are half human," she continued. "Your mind is being retrained in the Vulcan way,

so you may not understand feelings. But as my son, you have them."

Spock knew this. Like his father, Sarek, all Vulcans buried their feelings in logic. But Amanda was an Earthling. And she knew the computer was looking for Spock's human side.

"But I cannot wait here to find them," Spock said. "I must go to Earth to speak at Admiral Kirk's trial."

"You do this . . . for friendship?" Amanda asked with hope.

"I do this because I was there."

"Spock," she said, "You are alive because your feeling, human friends risked their lives for you."

Spock looked calmly at her. "Humans make illogical decisions."

Meanwhile, the space probe was reaching its destination—Earth.

Starfleet Command was in an uproar. Five of their vessels had been put out of order, and they could not get any others out of spacedock.

A frantic voice came over the intercom: "We have lost all internal power. Repeat, we have lost all power!"

At that moment, the space probe sent its strange sound into the Earth's oceans. And at Starfleet Command, all personnel stared helplessly at the view on their screens—the *sound* was turning the ocean water into huge clouds!

On Vulcan, everything was ready to go with the HMS *Bounty*. Scotty had even fixed the cloaking device, which the Klingons used to make the ship invisible.

As Kirk took his place on the bridge, Spock entered, wearing his Vulcan robe. "Permission to come aboard, Admiral," he said.

"Permission granted," Kirk answered. "And it's *Jim*, Spock, remember?"

"It would be improper to refer to you as Jim while you are in command, Admiral. Also, I must apologize. I seem to have misplaced my uniform."

"Well, you've been through a lot. Station, please."

As Spock walked to his station, both Kirk and McCoy noticed he looked stiff.

"You sure this is such a bright idea?" McCoy asked. "Spock isn't exactly working on all thrusters."

"It'll come back to him," Kirk answered—but even he wasn't so sure of that.

Soon the *Bounty* was ready. "Mr. Sulu, take us home," Kirk commanded.

Little did they know how important their trip was. At that moment, Earth was slowly

being covered by clouds. With the sun being blocked and all land being drenched with rain, the world would not be able to survive long.

As they got nearer to Earth, Uhura started to pick up an unknown distress signal. Spock listened in as Doctor McCoy approached him, smiling.

"Spock," McCoy said, "I just wanted to say it's nice to have your thoughts back in your head, not mine." Spock just stared back. "I mean, I may have carried your soul, but I sure couldn't fill your shoes."

"My shoes?"

"Forget it . . . " It was useless to make him feel anything, McCoy thought.

As McCoy walked away frustrated, Kirk ordered the distress signals put on screen. Most of what they saw was static, until the faint image of the Starfleet President ap-

peared. It was hard to tell what he was saying:

Warning: Do not approach Earth . . . orbiting probe . . . signals on energy wave unknown to us . . . wave directed at our oceans . . . all power sources have failed . . . starships powerless . . .

At that point the message began to clear. *A cloud envelope has covered the planet. Heavy rain and flooding. Temperatures dropping to critical level. Probe's signal has knocked out all channels. Communications may be impossible. . . . Save yourselves. Avoid the planet Earth. . . . Farewell.*

Shocked, Kirk had the probe's signal put on the speakers.

"Spock, what do you make of it?" Kirk asked.

"Most unusual. An unknown energy form of great intelligence and power. I find it illogical that it is hostile."

"Really?" McCoy interrupted, still sore at Spock. "You think it's just saying, 'Hi there' to the people on Earth?"

"There are other intelligent life forms on Earth, Doctor."

"You're suggesting it may be calling a life form other than man?" Kirk asked.

"A possibility. The President did say it was directed at the Earth's oceans."

The three men headed for the computer room to analyze the sound. Quickly, the computer came up with a picture of what the sound matched. Kirk's and McCoy's eyes widened when they saw it.

"As suspected," Spock said without emotion, "the probe's signals are the songs sung by whales. Specifically, humpback whales."

"That's crazy!" McCoy said. "Who would send a probe hundreds of light-years to talk to a whale?"

Kirk was deep in thought. "It's possible," he said. "Whales were on Earth far earlier than man."

"Ten million years earlier," Spock added. "Humpbacks were heavily hunted by man. They have been extinct since the twenty-first century. It is possible that aliens sent the probe to find out why they lost contact."

"Spock, could we imitate the humpback's answer to the call?"

"The sounds, but not the language."

"Then we must destroy the probe."

"Impossible. It would neutralize us easily."

"Is there no alternative?"

"Yes, but I cannot guarantee its success. We could attempt to find some humpback whales."

McCoy thought Spock was crazy. "You said there aren't any except on Earth of the past! So how . . . ?" Then he realized what Spock meant.

Time travel.

"Now wait a minute . . . " But McCoy was too late to argue.

"Spock, get the ship ready for a time warp," Kirk ordered.

Next stop—the cargo bay, where Kirk met Mr. Scott.

"Scotty, would we be able to fill this room with water?"

"I suppose so, sir. Are you planning to take a swim?"

"No, but we are going to find some humpback whales!"

"Whales? Admiral, how am I going to handle all that weight?"

"You'll work it out, Scotty. And remember—*two* of them!"

At Starfleet Command, workers ran about in a panic. Lightning and rain threatened to break through the room's huge window. But Admiral Cartwright and Sarek's attention was on the screen. A faint signal from Kirk was coming through.

Opinion . . . probe call . . . extinct spe-

cies, humpback whale . . . Starfleet—we
are going to attempt time travel.

That was the last they heard, as the
power went out. Cartwright and Sarek
stared silently at the blank screen.

"Good luck, Kirk," Sarek whispered.
"And all who go with you."

Suddenly there was a deafening crash.
The entire great window had blown inward,

and the room was instantly filled with flying objects, cries, and howling wind.

Kirk turned to Spock as he prepared the ship. "What is our target in time?"

"The late twentieth century."

The *Bounty* exploded into warp speed. They sped toward the sun, with heat shields at full power. Time travel was possible only if they could slingshot around the sun at Warp ten.

As they got nearer the sun, the bridge began to vibrate wildly.

"I don't think she'll hold together, Admiral!" Scotty shouted.

"No choice now, Scotty! Mr. Sulu, we need breakaway speed!"

"Warp nine point seven . . . point eight . . . breakaway speed . . . "

"Now, Sulu!"

Just as it seemed the ship would be swallowed by the sun, it blasted around like a white bullet.

Soon an image of the Earth filled the *Bounty*'s screen. "Judging by the air pollu-

tion, I believe we have arrived in the late
twentieth century," Spock reported. They
had done it!

To make the ship invisible, Commander
Chekov turned on the ship's cloaking device.

"Admiral," Uhura called out, "I am re-
ceiving whale songs from straight ahead—
San Francisco!"

Kirk was puzzled. "From a city? That
doesn't make sense."

Just then, Scotty's voice boomed over the speakers: "Admiral, you and Spock better get down here!"

Kirk and Spock rushed to the engine room. The ship's fuel, dilithium crystals, had become weak.

"We've got about twenty-four hours," said Scotty. "After that we'll be visible. And there'll be no way to get back home."

"Scotty, is there any way the dilithium can be recrystallized?" Kirk asked.

"Sorry, sir. We can't even do that in the twenty-third century."

Spock had an idea. "There *is* a twentieth-century possibility. But we need to collect photons from one of their nuclear reactors."

"Where would we find these reactors?" asked Kirk.

"Nuclear power was widely used in naval ships. . . . "

Kirk thought about this as they returned to the bridge. There, a nighttime view of San Francisco filled the viewing screen.

"Mr. Sulu, set us down in Golden Gate Park," Kirk ordered. "We'll divide into teams.

Chekov and Uhura are assigned to find the nuclear reactor. McCoy—you, Scotty, and Sulu will convert the cargo bay into a whale tank. Spock and I will try to trace these whale songs to their source."

They all agreed. But Kirk had one warning: "Be very careful. Try to fit in—many customs may take us by surprise. Remember, this is three hundred years in the past. These people have never seen an extraterrestrial before."

In reponse, Spock took a strip of lining out of his Vulcan robe. When he tied it around his head to cover up his pointed ears, he looked like a Japanese gentleman in samurai clothing.

"Mr. Chekov, give a phaser and a communicator to each team," Kirk continued. "We will only radio each other in an emergency. All right, let's do our job."

The *Bounty* landed in the park. The ship's ramp was visible when it let the crew out. But when it closed, nothing could be seen — except for the seven strangers from the twenty-third century.

They wandered onto the city streets and

looked around in wonder. Everything seemed so odd and ancient to them.

By the twenty-third century, money was not being used any more, but Kirk realized they needed some now. The only valuable thing he had was an antique pair of eyeglasses. At an antique shop he sold them to the owner for $200.

Kirk divided up the money with the crew, and the teams split off to their missions. Kirk had no idea where he and Spock should begin searching for the whales.

"Simple logic," said Spock. "I will read this map."

Posted on a bus stop nearby was a map of San Francisco. But Spock couldn't figure it out. Just then a bus pulled up. On its side was a large advertisement:

SEE GEORGE AND GRACIE

THE ONLY TWO HUMPBACK WHALES
IN CAPTIVITY

AT THE CETACEAN INSTITUTE,
SAUSALITO

"I think we'll find what we're looking for at the Cetacean Institute in Sausalito," said Kirk. "Two humpbacks named George and Gracie."

"How do you know this?"

Kirk gave a sly smile. "Simple logic."

When they reached the Institute, they were just in time for a tour. Kirk and Spock looked around in wonder at the main room. Huge models of whales hung from the ceiling.

Kirk noticed that the tour guide was an attractive woman. And from the look in her eyes, she noticed Kirk, too.

"Good morning. I'm Doctor Gillian Taylor and I'll be your guide," she began. "The Cetacean Institute is the world's only museum devoted just to whales. . . . Even though we have laws against whale hunting, some countries and pirates still kill them off. If this doesn't stop, there may soon be none left."

"To hunt animals to extinction is not logical," Spock said.

"Whoever said the human race was logical?" Gillian answered. "Now, if you'll follow me . . ."

She led them to the glass whale tank. They all stared down into it to see George and Gracie. In their time, Kirk and Spock had never seen Earth creatures so big.

Gillian looked at the whales with a smile.

"They wandered into San Francisco as babies and were brought here. Beautiful, aren't they? And intelligent, too. Why shouldn't they be? They're swimming around with the largest brains on Earth."

She led the group down the stairway that curved around the whale tank. No one noticed that Spock was not with them.

"Unfortunately, soon we will have to return George and Gracie to the open sea," Gillian said with a sigh. "For one thing, we can't afford to feed them a couple of tons of shrimp a day!"

Kirk was shocked. If they let the whales out to sea, how could his crew possibly find

them and beam them up in time? "How soon?" he asked.

"Soon," she answered sadly. "It's too bad, because I've grown quite fond of them."

At the bottom of the tank, the group looked at the whales through the glass.

Over speakers, a sound could be heard. "What you're hearing is a whale song, sung by the male. In the ocean, other whales will pick up the song and pass it on."

Suddenly Kirk's eyes popped open. In the whale tank he saw *three* figures—George and Gracie, and *Spock*, with his hand on one of the whales.

He's reading the whale's mind, Kirk thought.

"We still don't know the reason for the songs," Gillian continued.

An older woman spoke up. "Maybe he's singing to the man."

Gillian spun around to see Spock. "What the—!" She raced to the top of the tank, and Kirk followed.

When they got there, Spock had come out of the water. Gillian was furious at him and Kirk. "I don't know what this is about," she said, "but I want you guys out of here right now or I call the cops!"

The two men quickly left the building. "What did you learn from them, Spock?" Kirk asked.

"They are very unhappy about the way whales have been treated by man."

"Do you think they'll help us?"

"I believe I was successful in telling them what we wanted." Not the answer Kirk hoped for, but good enough.

Beep-beep. Kirk answered a signal on his communicator.

"Admiral, this is Chekov. We have found the ship with the nuclear reactor, and it's called . . . the *Enterprise.*"

At the Institute things had quieted down. Gillian sat by the edge of the whale tank, while the whales sprayed her and made noises. It sounded like they were trying to tell her something. But what?

Before long, Gillian noticed her boss come in. "Bob . . . it's tearing me apart," she said. "I don't want to let the whales go."

"I know, but we can't keep them here without risking their lives." He gave her a friendly look. "You look tired. Why don't you go home?"

She nodded and left. In a few minutes, an assistant came in.

"We all ready?" he asked.

"Looks like it," Bob answered.

"Gillian's gonna go crazy."

"I know, but it's for her own good." Something sneaky was up.

On her drive home, Gillian passed by Kirk and Spock and offered them a ride.

Kirk whispered to Spock, "It's her—from the Institute. Maybe we can find out when those whales are really leaving."

Both men climbed into the car. As they drove off, Gillian asked, "What were you guys trying to do back there? Was it some kind of macho thing?"

"Can I ask *you* something?" Kirk said. "What's going to happen when you release the whales?"

"They're gonna have to take their

chances. They'll be at risk from hunters. . . .
Say, you guys aren't from the military, are
you?"

"No, ma'am," Kirk said.

Just then, Spock spoke up. "Gracie is
pregnant."

Gillian jammed on the brakes in anger,
and the car skidded to a stop. "All right. How
do you know that? And who are you?"

"We can't tell you," Kirk said. "All I can
say is we mean no harm to the whales. In
fact, we may be able to help you—in ways
you couldn't possibly imagine."

"Or believe," Gillian said.

"Very likely. You know, maybe we ought
to talk about this over dinner."

Gillian agreed, and she drove them all to
a restaurant.

Miles away, Scotty, McCoy, and Sulu
were at a Plexiglas factory called Plexicorp.
Their mission: to find a material that would
make a good whale tank for the *Bounty.* Sulu
had split off to look at the factory's helicop-

ter. And Scotty and McCoy had gotten inside
the factory by pretending Scotty was an important professor from Scotland.

Doctor Nichols, the factory director,
showed the two men into his office.

Scotty knew he needed to get a lot of Plexiglas from Doctor Nichols. But what could he give him in return? He thought a moment and then said, "Doctor Nichols, let's say you have a big wall of Plexiglas that's six inches thick, to hold tons of water. Suppose I could show you a way to make a wall just as strong but only *one* inch thick. Would that be worth something to you?"

"Are you joking?"

"He never jokes," McCoy said with a serious face.

Scotty sat in front of a nearby computer. With incredible speed, the screen glowed with graphics that amazed Nichols. He knew he could become rich and famous with this formula. Now he would give *anything* to "Professor" Scotty.

Meanwhile, Kirk had asked Gillian to drive into Golden Gate Park—to the landing site of the invisible *Bounty*. When they got there, Spock stepped out.

"You won't change your mind?" Gillian asked him.

Spock didn't understand the slang. "Is there something wrong with the one I have?" he asked.

"Just a little joke," Kirk said to Gillian. "See you later, Spock."

But Gillian had another question for Spock. "How did you know Gracie was pregnant? Nobody knows that."

"Gracie does," Spock said. He turned to

Kirk. "I'll be right here." With that, he walked away.

"He's just going to hang around the bushes while we eat?" Gillian asked.

Kirk shrugged. "It's his way."

Spock waited until the car pulled away. Then, when no one was around, he quietly beamed out.

Kirk and Gillian drove to a restaurant and sat down for dinner. Kirk began asking questions. "Exactly how will George and Gracie be taken away?"

"They'll be flown to Alaska and released there." Gillian sighed sadly. "We'll keep in

touch with them by tagging them with radio transmitters."

Kirk looked deeply into her eyes. "You know, I could take those whales someplace where they wouldn't be hunted."

Gillian laughed. "You? You can't even get around without a lift!" But there was something about Kirk. He didn't look like a liar—and she liked him. "Where could you take them?"

Kirk spoke carefully. "It's not so much a matter of *place* as of *time*."

Gillian was listening in hopes that Kirk had an answer. But suddenly Kirk's communicator beeped—and that broke the spell.

Kirk flipped it open. "What is it?" he shouted. "I told you never to call—"

"Sorry, Admiral," came Scotty's voice. "We thought you'd like to know, we're beaming them in now."

"I see," Kirk said. "Tell them phasers on stun. Good luck. Kirk out."

Gillian looked at him sharply. "Who *are* you?"

"All right, the *truth*. . . . I'm from the late twenty-third century. I've been sent back in time to bring two humpback whales with me in order to . . . bring them back from extinction."

"Well, why didn't you say so? Why all the disguises?"

"You want details?"

"I wouldn't miss this for anything."

"Then tell me when the whales are leaving."

"OK, your friend was right. Gracie is *very* pregnant. At noon tomorrow the whales get shipped out—and I'm sure all the newspaper and TV people will be there."

Kirk jumped up from the table. "Noon tomorrow? Come on. I don't have much time."

As they drove to Golden Gate Park, Kirk told her all about his crew and his mission.

"Well, that is the craziest story I ever heard," Gillian said as they pulled up to the invisible ship's landing site.

"Now, will you tell me something?" said Kirk. "George and Gracie's transmitters. How can we get in touch with them?"

"I can't tell you. That's top secret."

"Look. I can get two other humpbacks

from the open sea. But I'd rather take yours. It would be better for me, better for you— and better for them. If you change your mind, this is where I'll be."

Gillian looked around. "Here . . . in the park?"

"Right." He gave her a kiss and walked off.

Just as Gillian started her car, she heard a funny noise. She turned around.

There was no one within yards of where Kirk had been standing.

On board the *Bounty*, Spock reported to Kirk, "The tank will be finished by morning."

"What about Uhura and Chekov?"

"We're waiting for their call."

"If we don't move quickly we'll lose the whales!"

"In that case, chances are our mission would fail."

"Our *mission*?!" Kirk was furious at Spock's calmness. "Spock, you're talking about the end of every life on Earth! You're half human—haven't you got any feelings about *that*?"

As Kirk stormed off, Spock looked like he did have feelings—anger, pain, and confusion.

In the Naval Base, Uhura and Chekov had sneaked into the USS *Enterprise*. They quietly collected photons near the nuclear reactor. When they finished, Uhura radioed Scotty and asked him to beam them up.

"My transporter power's very low," Scot-

ty replied. "I got to bring you in one at a time. Stand by."

"Take the collector. You go first!" Chekov said. He stepped aside as Uhura was beamed out.

Suddenly Chekov heard the sound of running feet. Guards!

"Freeze!" a gruff voice called out.

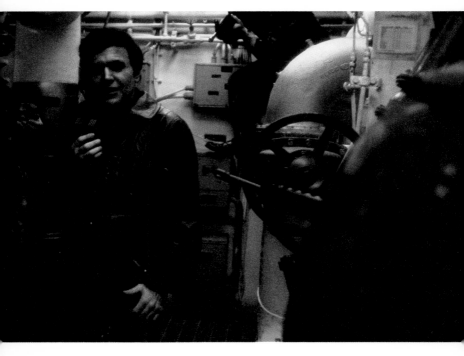

It was too late to be beamed up. The guards took Chekov to their office. Soon the room was filled with naval officers and FBI agents.

One agent started firing questions at Chekov. "All right, who are you and what are you doing here?"

"My name is Pavel Chekov, Starfleet

Lieutenant Commander, United Federation of Planets."

"He's a Russian," someone said. "We better call Washington."

Quickly, Chekov snatched up his phaser. "Don't move or I will have to stun you."

The FBI agent came toward him. Chekov fired.

But the phaser made a tiny noise and did nothing.

"Must be the radiation," Chekov said. He raced out the nearest door.

The chase was on. Chekov climbed a ladder onto the deck of the *Enterprise.* But

Marines and patrolmen came at him from all directions. He stopped by the edge of the deck, trapped.

There *had* to be a way to escape. He looked to his left. A group of Marines came at him. Chekov slipped—right off the edge of the ship!

When Chekov's chasers looked over the edge, they saw him lying on a barge floating on the water. His eyes were closed.

Things were tense on the *Bounty*. They had lost touch with Chekov, and Uhura felt terrible that she had left him alone.

"Uhura, you did what was necessary. Keep trying," Kirk said gently. Then he spoke into the intercom. "Mr. Scott, how long for the dilithium crystals?"

"It'll be well into tomorrow."

"Not good enough, Scotty. You've got to do better!"

The next morning, Gillian drove up to the Cetacean Institute. She was surprised— no cameras, no newspapermen. She unlocked the main door and walked into the tank area.

George and Gracie were gone.

Gillian saw her boss standing in the corner of the room. "They left last night," he said. "We didn't want a mob scene with the press. Besides, we thought it would be easier on you this way."

Gillian's face turned red with anger.

"You . . . sent them away. Without even letting me say good-bye?" She slapped him and ran outside. Crying, she jumped into her car and drove to the place where she left Kirk in Golden Gate Park.

"*Kirk*!" she screamed. But her voice was drowned out by a loud sound in the air. She looked up to see Sulu in a helicopter. He was

lowering a huge sheet of Plexiglas into . . .
thin air!

Then she saw something that made her
jaw drop open. Scotty was floating in the air,
guiding Sulu. But there was only half of him
there! She couldn't know that the other half
of him was being covered by an invisible
ship.

"Kirk!" she yelled. "I need you!"

On board the ship, Kirk heard her. And in a moment, Gillian noticed *herself* start to disappear!

In a moment she was aboard the *Bounty*, facing Kirk. "Hello, Alice," he said. "Welcome to Wonderland."

"It's *true* . . . what you said . . ."

Kirk showed her the new whale tanks.

"Kirk," she said, "They're gone."

"Gone?!"

"They were taken last night. I wasn't told. They're in Alaska by now."

Just then, Spock came in and said, "Admiral, we have full power. . . . Hello, Doctor, welcome aboard."

As Gillian stared at Spock's pointy ears, Uhura's voice came in on the intercom.

"Admiral . . . I've found Chekov. He's in emergency surgery."

"Uhura! Where?"

"At Mercy Hospital. They don't think he'll live!"

In an instant, Kirk, McCoy, and Gillian were in Mercy Hospital. They found hospital uniforms and a bed with wheels. Kirk and McCoy dressed as doctors and Gillian put on a nurse's uniform. She jumped under the bedsheets and pretended to be a patient— and off they went.

They wheeled their way past doctors and policemen, right into the operating room.

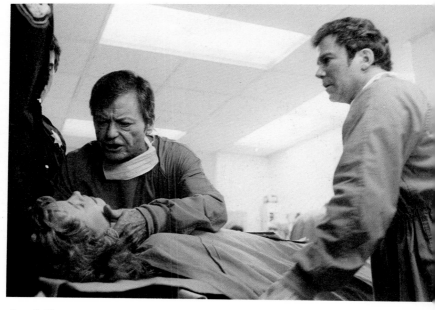

And there, unconscious on a bed, was Chekov. A doctor and two nurses were around
him.

When no one was looking, Gillian sat up.
She, McCoy, and Kirk all put on white masks
and went over to Chekov. McCoy examined
Chekov with his tricorder.

"Hey, what do you think you're doing?"
the doctor said.

"I must get to work on him right away

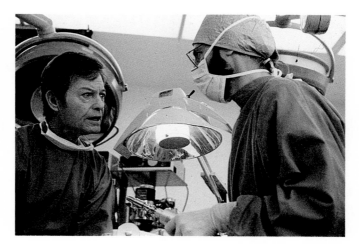

or he'll die!" McCoy answered. "So put away your butcher knives and let me save this man!"

"I don't know who you are," the doctor said, "but I'm going to have you removed!"

"Doctors, please," Kirk said. And with one swift move, he had his phaser drawn.

Kirk then aimed his phaser at the doctor and nurses, and pointed them into a small room. He shut the door, fired his phaser at the lock—and melted it!

At the same time, McCoy began to heal Chekov with his tricorder. "Wake up, man, wake up," he said.

Kirk and Gillian joined McCoy. Soon Chekov's eyes started to flutter. He sat up with a start. "Doctor McCoy!" he said.

McCoy smiled. "Hello, Chekov."

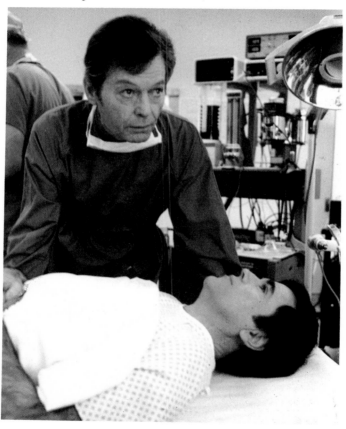

They wheeled Chekov out of the operating room and down the hall. One of the policemen remembered seeing them when they went in. "How's the patient?" he asked.

"He's gonna make it!" Kirk answered.

The policeman looked at his partner. "*He*? They went in with a *she*!"

Oops. Kirk, McCoy, and Gillian raced away, pushing Chekov on the bed. Close behind them were the hospital guards, with their weapons in hand. At the end of the hall a large elevator door opened, and Kirk rolled the bed right in.

The door closed, and Gillian felt them going the wrong way. "We're going up!" she cried out. "They'll take the stairs and catch us!"

"Calm yourself, Nurse," Kirk replied. He pulled out his communicator. "Scotty, get us out of here."

When the elevator got to the top floor, the guards were waiting. The door opened and they stared in shock. No one was there.

At that moment, the four runaways beamed in near the *Bounty* landing site.

McCoy and Chekov went aboard, but Kirk stayed outside with Gillian.

"I'm coming with you," she said.

"You can't. Our next stop is the twenty-third century. Just tell me how to contact the whales. Give me their radio frequency."

"All right—401 megahertz."

"Thank you . . . for everything," Kirk said. Then he spoke into his communicator. "Beam me up, Scotty."

Kirk started to disappear, but Gillian grabbed him by the waist.

When he beamed on board, Gillian was with him. She grinned. "Surprise!"

Kirk was angry, but he didn't have time to argue. The dilithium crystals were back to normal, so he rushed to the bridge and ordered the ship to take off. As the bridge whirred into action, Gillian looked around, amazed.

The *Bounty* flew over San Francisco, on course to Alaska.

Kirk spoke into the intercom. "Scotty, are the whale tanks ready?"

"Aye," Scotty answered. "But I've never beamed up four hundred tons before."

"*Four hundred* tons?"

"It ain't just the whales, it's the water."

Just then the whale's radio signal was heard.

"That's it!" Gillian shouted.

"Put them on screen," Kirk commanded.

Instantly the screen showed George and Gracie in the ocean, jumping and singing like two happy children.

"Admiral," said Uhura, "I'm picking up another signal in the area." On the screen flashed a picture of a ship.

"It's a whaling ship!" Gillian cried.

"How far from the whales, Uhura?" Kirk asked.

"About one nautical mile."

"Oh no, we're too late!" Gillian cried.

The invisible spaceship was in a race against the whale hunters. It sliced through the sky, as the hunters began loading their harpoons.

"Ten seconds, sir," Sulu said.

The hunters lined up the whales in their targets—and fired! The harpoons sailed through the air.

But . . . *THWANG!* The hunters couldn't

believe what they saw. Their harpoons seemed to hit something invisible and fall into the water.

And they practically jumped out of their pants at what happened next. The *Bounty*, big as a football field, suddenly appeared right where the harpoons had hit! The hunters spun around in a panic—and beat it.

The *Bounty* crew cheered. But the biggest problem was still ahead. Kirk again spoke into the intercom.

"Mr. Scott. Let's try to beam those whales in!"

"I'll give it me best, sir."

In the cargo bay, Scotty was sweating. The transporter groaned with the strain. "Stay with me, sir," Scotty said, "I need more power curve. . . . five seconds . . . four . . . three . . . two . . . one!"

Before his eyes, the two huge whales slowly appeared. And around them was half a tank of seawater. Scotty's mouth opened in amazement.

"Admiral!" he called. "There be whales here!"

"Well done, Scotty!" Kirk answered. "Prepare for warp speed as soon as possible."

With a blast of power, the *Bounty* left Earth for outer space.

Kirk stood up. "Mr. Sulu, take control. I'm taking our guest down to see her whales. Mr. Spock, we're traveling with a lot of added weight. Have you figured out how we can get enough speed for time travel?"

"Mr. Scott cannot give me exact figures, Admiral. So I will . . . make a guess."

"You? A *guess*?" Kirk laughed. "Spock, that's wonderful!"

As Kirk and Gillian left, McCoy said to Spock, "That means he feels safer about your 'guesses' than most other people's facts."

Spock felt complimented. "Then I will make the best guess I can."

Meanwhile, Kirk and Gillian joined Scotty by the whale tank. "Hard to imagine," Kirk said. "When Man was killing these creatures, he was destroying his own future." He looked at Gillian. "You know, our chances of getting home are not good. You should have stayed where you belong."

"I belong here," she said. "After all, if you do get back home, who in your century knows anything about humpback whales?"

"You have a point . . ."

At that moment, the ship began to vibrate.

"We're having some power fall-off, sir," Scotty said.

Kirk rushed to the bridge, leaving Scotty and Gillian behind. When he got there, Scotty's voice boomed over the intercom: "Warp seven point nine. . . . Mr. Sulu, that's all I can give you!"

"Spock, can we make breakaway speed?" Kirk said.

"No, Admiral. We may be pulled into the sun. However, there is a chance if I can change our path."

"Warp eight point one," Sulu said. "Maximum speed, sir!"

"Admiral, I need thruster control," said Spock.

"Acceleration thrusters when Spock commands!" Kirk ordered.

Spock concentrated on his controls, waiting for the right moment. "Steady . . . steady. . . . *Now.*"

The ship shot toward the sun. Then, silence. It seemed the ship had been swallowed up.

But sure enough, with a bang of retro rockets, the *Bounty* whipped around the other side. They were out of danger. Before long, the ship slowed down to normal speed.

But something was terribly wrong. There was no sound at all on the bridge. No engines, no beeps—nothing.

Suddenly, they could hear the gibberish of the probe.

"Spock, where are we?!" Kirk asked.

"I don't know, Admiral. Computers are not working."

"I have no control, sir!" said Sulu.

"Picture, Uhura!"

"I can't, sir—nothing!"

Kirk didn't know what to do. The entire crew was helpless.

"For heaven's sake, Jim, where are we?" McCoy said. The probe's noise got louder, and they all sensed they were falling.

And they *were*—right toward the Golden Gate Bridge in San Francisco!

But this was twenty-third century San Francisco, at the exact moment they had left it. And at that moment, the window was crashing in on the Starfleet Federation Headquarters—just as it did before. Sarek and Cartwright stared helplessly.

Then a look of horror crossed their faces as they saw Kirk's ship narrowly miss the Golden Gate Bridge and crash into the bay.

The ship's windows blew out, and all crew members went flying around the bridge. As they started to sink, Kirk yelled to Spock, "Open the hatch!"

Spock obeyed him. Kirk looked through the hatch and into the rain. "You got us to the right place, Spock. Now all we have to do is get the whales out before we sink." He

turned to leave the bridge and said, "Mr. Spock, see to the safety of all hands."

Kirk fought his way down to the cargo bay. He ripped open the door to find Scotty

and Gillian up to their necks in water. He helped them up into the corridor.

"The whales, Scotty?" Kirk shouted.

"Stuck! There's no power to the bay doors!"

"The explosive override? Let's blow it open!"

"It's underwater! There's no way to reach it!"

"Go on ahead! Close the hatch!" Kirk took a deep breath and dove underwater. He couldn't find it. He swam back to the surface, gasped for air, and went back down. Now he saw what he was looking for. This was their last chance. He tore open a seal and pressed a button.

BA-ROOM!—an underwater explosion. The cargo bay doors swung open—and Kirk swam out through them. His air was running out. He raced to the surface. Just as he was about to pass out, his head popped above the water. He looked around to see his crew members hanging onto the top of the sinking ship—including Gillian.

For a minute he was relieved—until he heard the nagging sound of the probe. Where were the whales? Kirk dove back underwater. He swam toward the cargo bay until a wonderful sight made him stop. Coming out of the bay doors into the ocean were George and Gracie.

Kirk swam back to the surface and grabbed onto the ship. But the rain was falling harder than ever, and the probe's call was not being answered.

"Why don't they sing?!" Kirk said.

And then, all of a sudden, it happened. From deep in the ocean came the song of George the whale.

The probe stopped. Then it turned its antenna toward the sound. It began its signal again, this time softer. The whale and the probe were talking to each other!

It went on for a while, each song answered by the signal. And when they were through, the probe blasted into outer space.

All at once, the rain stopped, the clouds parted—and the sun began to peek through.

At Starfleet Command, the lights came back on. "Mr. President," Admiral Cartwright cried, "we have power!"

The President looked out at the bay and saw the sinking spaceship. "Send a rescue shuttle!"

Within seconds, Kirk and his crew heard the sound of their rescuers on the way.

"Congratulations, Jim," said McCoy

with a big smile. "I think you've saved the Earth."

"Not me, Bones," answered Kirk. "*They* did it."

The crew looked out to sea. George and Gracie were jumping and spouting happily in their new world. And above them, as the sun broke through the clouds, was the most beautiful rainbow they'd ever seen.

But when things got back to normal, there was still a big problem left: the trial of the *Enterprise* crew. Into the Federation Council Chamber walked Kirk, McCoy, Scotty, Uhura, Sulu, and Chekov to be judged by the President. In the front row of the audience were Gillian, Sarek, and Spock. When the crew took their places on the stand, Spock rose and joined them.

"Captain Spock," the President said, "you do not stand accused."

"I stand with my shipmates," Spock answered. "Their fate shall be mine."

"As you wish." The President read the list of crimes—attacking Federation officers,

stealing and destroying the Starship *Enterprise*, and disobeying the orders of the Starfleet Commander.

Kirk knew he had done it all for a good cause—saving Spock's life. But still, all the charges were true. "On behalf of us all, Mr. President, I plead guilty."

But the President surprised them. Because of what Kirk and his crew had done to save Earth, he threw away all the charges—except one.

"The remaining charge—disobeying a superior officer—is directed only at Admiral Kirk. James T. Kirk, I hereby reduce you to the rank of Captain." The crowd didn't know how to take this. "And," the President continued, "because of your new rank, you will be given the duties for which you have shown greatest ability: command of a starship."

Kirk was shocked. This was exactly what he wanted—his own starship again!

"Captain Kirk," the President said, "your new command awaits you. You and your crew have saved this planet from its own mistake. And we forever thank you."

The audience broke into a standing ovation.

As the crowd left, Gillian kissed Kirk and said good-bye.

"Where are you going?" he said.

"You're going to your ship, I'm going to mine. A science vessel. I've got three hundred years of catching up to do. Don't worry, I'll be in touch. See you round the galaxy!"

Kirk shook his head and smiled.

❖

At the same time, Sarek was saying good-bye to his son, Spock.

"I am impressed with you and your associates, Spock."

"They are my friends," Spock said.

"Yes, of course. . . . Do you have any message for your mother?"

Spock thought for a moment. Then he said, "Tell her I feel fine. . . ." His human side was, after all, coming back. And he knew his mother would want to know he could finally answer the last question of his memory test.

Later, a shuttle craft picked up Kirk and his crew to take them to their ship.

"Probably an old bucket of bolts," said McCoy.

But he was wrong—very wrong. They came closer to the ship. In a minute they could see the whole thing. One by one, their faces lit up.

It was the *Enterprise*! A shiny, new ship built to be exactly like the one the crew had commanded for so many years.

"My friends," Kirk said, "we've come home."

The great doors of the ship opened and

the crew stepped aboard. They went straight
to the bridge and took their old places.

Kirk sat in his captain's chair. "Let's see
what she's got, Mr. Sulu."

In a flash, the *Enterprise* hit warp speed,
on the first of its new voyages.